Shackleford Banks Sasquatch

by

Christopher Flowers

For everyone who was involved with Uwharrie.
You know who you are.

Chapter 1

Tom didn't believe in bigfoot.

When he set up camp on the beach that evening, his thoughts were fixed on the rhythmic static of the waves some fifty feet away. He thought about the Atlantic, an infinite, black plane that seemed to thrum under the eastern North Carolina moon. Sure, he considered the possibility of minor inconveniences; a stray speckled crab slipping into his tent, for example, sidelong and scouring the sand for bits of algae. He thought about the feral horses that occupied this island, but knew that, really, they were harmless. There was also the salt smell that permeated everything; a pleasant reminder of his current location at the junction of two worlds. He chewed on cold pizza and considered how remarkable it was that his day had ended here, on Shackleford Island, a place so distant from the ever-expanding sprawl of Charlotte.

Tom certainly didn't think that, from beyond the rippling cattails, a humanoid creature seven-and-a-half feet tall was waiting for him to fall asleep so that it could slip in and steal the scraps from his subpar dinner.

There wasn't much to claim; Tom was careful to package his leftover pizza crusts in two plastic Food Lion grocery bags, carefully tucking them away in the front pouch of his backpack. Still, the smell of heavily baked dough floated away from the tent and found the flaring nostrils of the starving animal.

The creature had survived by collecting scraps for a long time. Its diet mostly consisted of stale crackers or a partially discarded ham sandwich, with the occasional decaying flounder or a handful of squirming sand fiddlers thrown into the mix.

Once, in an unimaginable stroke of luck, it had found an artificial box filled with delights: a half-eaten Baby Ruth, an unopened packet of Cheez-Its, and an apple. After gorging itself, the creature studied the hard, blue material; he was fascinated by the way the stark white top of the container flapped up and down like a jaw. The box had been borderline incomprehensible, but, he surmised, it must have come from a human, like the one now sleeping in this flimsily constructed nest.

As the beast approached the man's tent, it drew in a deep breath. Sand gnats circled its salt-hardened hair. It was a master of stealth: nothing more than a shadow, hunched and intentional, as stout as a redwood and equally noiseless.

The animal could hear the man breathing. The human was snoring, in fact, and his warble almost matched the steady pounding of the surf. The creature peeled back the flap, and his nose told him that the strange lump of cloth barely visible in a far corner of the construct was where he would find his prize.

A sturdy gust scraped across the tide and made its way to Tom. With a shiver, he sat bolt upright, one arm still tangled in the orange fabric of his sleeping bag.

For a moment, nothing happened. It was midnight black in the tent, an inky pitch that was momentarily all-consuming. The moon had become partially obscured by a drifting cloud bank, and Tom's eyes had trouble adjusting. The creature, though, was built for this. It was three feet from Tom, and it looked directly into his eyes. It mostly scavenged, but its species had learned to hunt when the necessity arose. The animal was silent beyond measure and possessed horrific strength. It could think, this beast. It could reason. In the end, though, it was a primal entity driven by primal needs.

The creature observed that the man's eyes weren't like his. That is to say, they weren't large and tinged with concentric shades of brown, able to cut through the darkest nights with ease. Tom's eyes were blue and small; unreflective and unremarkable. It was a wonder, the creature thought, that this thing can see anything at all. The beast had experienced eyes like this before, and the memory of that encounter reawakened a deep anger.

Tom had the spine-chilling sense that he was not alone. Something was in the tent. He tried to slow his breathing and thought briefly about pretending that he had started from a dream. Tom considered gently retreating to the comfort of the sleeping bag, pretending he was aware of nothing. He knew, though, this wasn't possible. Whoever–or whatever–it was that peered at him knew that the man had been alerted to its presence.

Was it a horse? He tried to convince himself this was the answer. Yes: a horse had smelled his food, and it had wandered into his campsite. Horses were all over this island. Everything that made Tom human, though, told him this wasn't right.

"Hello?" The word barely escaped his mouth as a whisper. Tom accidentally swallowed the "o" that trailed the "Hell" and cleared his throat, preparing for a second attempt.

"Hello." This time the word emerged as a statement.

The creature had slowed its breathing to the point that there was no possibility a dull thing like this human could perceive the ebb and flow of its chest. This animal could see Tom's eyes adjusting to the scant light and realized the time it had available to act was dwindling. Suddenly remembering its size in relation to this curious intruder, the animal decided to lunge for the pack. It drew in a deep breath, extended a massive, furry arm, and snatched the bundle. When the creature stood, the tent came with it.

Silhouetted by the disc of the moon, Tom saw the monster in full.

"Jesus. JESUS!"

The creature heard the man's speech, and it was a familiar cadence. There was a melody to it, and, despite the animal's slowly gestating rage, this generated curiosity. The beast stooped and drew closer to Tom, who backpedaled and tripped on the rigging of his tent. Trying to right himself, Tom reached out instinctively, grabbing one of the straps that dangled from the creature's tight grip on his backpack.

When the man grabbed at the monster's prize, a fury that had been long dormant inside the animal was uncaged. A shade of red descended over its vision. It was the sense that this thing, this human–this competitor–was trying to reclaim the food; the sustenance it now cradled and had so carefully worked to secure. He remembered other humans who had attempted far worse.

The creature dropped the backpack.

Tom continued his own version of a frantic crabwalk, spidering backward toward the line of dunes hovering near his campsite. But the creature was fast; before Tom was able to process the speed with which five coarse fingers closed around his wrist, he found himself floating over the sand, looking directly into the face of the towering beast.

The smell was overwhelming. There was a stench that rolled from the creature's mouth with each ragged breath. Was this a mutated gorilla? Tom considered the options, scrambling for some kind of logic to help rationalize the scene. Slowly, the reality of the encounter dawned on him. This wasn't an ape. It wasn't a bear. It wasn't anything that should exist at all.

Tears carved glistening trails on Tom's face.

"Bigfoot." He muttered the word in an absentminded attempt to bring order to chaos.

The creature held Tom like a freshly caught fish that dangled from a line, slowly drawing the man closer to his face. After a long, deep breath, the animal released a primordial roar. Then, positioning its other massive hand along Tom's ribs, the creature tightened its grip and yanked.

Tom fell to the sand like a brick. Glad to be free, he stumbled to his feet and ran in the direction he'd come from that same afternoon, toward the ferry drop-off, in the vain hope that someone else would hear his panicked screams. As he pumped his arms, pain overcame the adrenaline that had fueled his will to escape. He came to a slow trot and stopped. Dazed, Tom turned to examine his right arm to determine what, exactly, the creature had done. Where the crook of his forearm and elbow should have been was an unobstructed view of the late-night beach, broken shells strewn among sharp grass.

His arm was gone.

Turning as far as his neck would allow, Tom saw a tattered mound of flesh at his shoulder. Blood oozed quietly down his turquoise T-shirt in the pale moonlight. There was the strange sensation that he could flex the fingers of his right hand; bend his arm into a V and make contact with the gaping wound. It was a phantom tingling that caused delirium. Still, the cascading pain that gathered at his collarbone told him to continue his flight to civilization. Just as he'd collected himself and channeled his faculties so that all his energy was focused on putting one foot in front of the other, the creature appeared. It blotted out the white circle of moon, legs spread wide, hemming Tom into the narrow path that led away from the pendulum boom of distant swells.

Whimpering, Tom dropped to his knees.

"You're not real. You can't be real."

The creature bent forward, and Tom could see that the hair lining its mouth was caked in the same dark crimson that had erupted from his shoulder. Still holding the severed arm, the beast took a large bite from the bicep. The wet sound of chewing caused Tom to drift toward unconsciousness.

Tom squeezed his eyes shut, and he felt his body being lifted from the cold sand in a parabolic arc. When he blinked for the final time, he found that he was peering skyward, toward a tapestry of stars. The clap of a distant thundercloud mingled with a roiling shore gust, and Tom's shrieks dissolved among the herd of horses that grazed mutely among the reeds.

Chapter 2

Erica wasn't one to worry, but when Tom didn't complete his usual text message check-in that Saturday morning, she knew something was wrong. They were a family of habits: Tom washed the dishes after every meal (even if he cooked), carefully squaring the freshly washed kitchen hand towel atop the small counter space next to the stove. And he always—no matter where he was or what he was doing—sent a "Love you" text message to Erica the morning after embarking on a trip.

The customary response, of course, was "I know." They were Star Wars fans, and their dialogue frequently went something like this: "Tom, please, how many times have I said it: put the Ketchup on the second shelf in the fridge door." Tom would murmur a reply: "I'm altering the deal. Pray I don't alter it any further." Erica would produce a halfhearted smile, sigh, and drop the request until it was resurrected that same afternoon. This was their pattern.

When she called Tom and got nothing but a voicemail greeting, she contacted Michael. Tom and Michael had grown up together, and, other than Erica, Michael knew Tom better than anyone else. She assumed he'd offer some kind of reassurance. After all, Tom was bad at remembering things. One time he left a freshly unboxed iPad on top of his car while stuffing an armload of groceries in the backseat. Then Tom drove away, oblivious to the $800 mistake. The small slab of technology presumably is still wedged in someone's front bumper on Interstate 77, like some kind of new-age ninja star.

"Well, that is weird." This isn't the response Erica had hoped for. "I'll call him."

When Michael didn't receive a response, he shrugged and said, "Let's give it a few hours. The signal there is probably terrible. I think there was some weather in the area, too."

This made sense, and it calmed Erica enough for her to muddle through her morning routine of downing two cups of coffee with one dash of French Vanilla creamer each. Once she'd logged into work from her home office, she entered what Tom referred to as "the zone"; she was completely immersed in spreadsheets and pivot tables for the next few hours. It was only when her stomach grumbled that Erica realized the time and became increasingly unsettled. She checked her cell: Tom hadn't called or texted. She thought, "maybe he lost his phone," but Erica knew that theory didn't hold water. Even though he loved the outdoors–especially his beloved Crystal Coast beaches–Tom cared deeply about his friends and family, and he wouldn't want anyone to worry. He would have hopped the morning ferry and made his way to an AT&T store to pick up (at the very least) a cheap replacement.

Michael showed up at Erica's around 3:30 that afternoon, his car loaded with camping gear and several sets of clothes.

"I decided to call in and let them know I won't be there on Monday or Tuesday." Michael didn't particularly love his job working as a phone operator for a burgeoning medical equipment outfit, and he wished he'd taken Tom up on his offer to join him for a weekend of sun, sand, and, well, junk food. Tom never ate well on these trips, but they seemed to rekindle his soul in a way that a biweekly outing to a brewery couldn't.

"Maybe you should call the police down there, too. I don't know. I don't want to freak you out, but it's weird that he hasn't checked in. Tell them that I'm headed there and to keep an eye out for him."

The notion that Erica might need to alert the local authorities had been rattling around in the back of her skull for several hours.

"Look, I'll probably get there tonight and find him in a bar or something. I'm sure we're making a mountain out of a molehill."

Erica grinned and nodded.

"Thanks, Mike."

Michael didn't love the nickname, but because Tom used it–and Erica was basically family–he didn't object.

"Try not to worry. I'll let you know when I get there."

They hugged, and Michael quickly made his way toward the Kia hatchback that would whisk him along Highway 74 and into the flat terrain beyond Raleigh. With a final wave he was off. Erica pulled the front door shut, the number to the Carteret County Sheriff's Office already punched into her phone.

*   *   *

It was 9:09 PM when Michael arrived in Beaufort. Even though it was a perfectly clear Saturday evening, the place was a ghost town. The ferry wouldn't depart until 8:30 the next morning, and the AirBnB he had booked earlier in the day was a two-bedroom rowhouse that was positioned against a ramshackle bar called BOB's. A comically large red and white fishing bobber served as the apostrophe, and the letters were fixed to a piece of warped pine that was positioned over the entrance. "Might as well start there," Michael concluded. "If Tom's anywhere in this town that's still open, it's got to be this place."

After keying in the door code and dropping off his duffel bag, Michael approached the building, a neon "MILLER LITE" sign casting a pink haze on the pavement. He shouldered his way through the door, which seemed too large to fit its frame.

Inside he found a smattering of patrons. Muffled conversation crowded the small tavern, and he quietly made his way to an open stool. A woman with iron gray hair approached him, offering an obligatory smile. "Hey there. What can I get you?"

Michael gave the chalkboard overhead a cursory glance and settled on Red Oak (an oddly highbrow option for a dive like this). He placed his order and surveyed the room.

The folks here were clearly blue collar. By the looks of it they had worked long days, and whatever waited for them at home probably wasn't pleasant. When the bartender returned with a glass of amber beer, Michael did what he could to engage her in conversation.

"I just drove in from Charlotte. My buddy Tom got here yesterday; took the ferry to Shackleford, and the damn fool isn't answering anyone's calls."

She shrugged and placed her hands flat on the uneven surface of the bar.

"The cell service out there is hit and miss."

"You're probably right." Michael felt the cool of the glass, the condensation already gathering along its circumference.

"I'm guessing the name doesn't ring a bell, then. He hasn't been here?"

Michael took a heavy swig from the glass. The woman wrinkled her nose and thought for a second.

"Tom, wasn't it?"

"Yeah. He's about my height. There's a little gray in his hair, and he's clearly not from around here."

The woman laughed and moved a rag across the bar in slow circles.

"Haven't seen him, honey. I'm here every day and I'm good with names and faces."

Michael drained his glass and placed a crisp ten dollar bill on the counter. "Thanks. I really appreciate it." Before standing, he paused and raised a finger. "I'm so sorry–what is your name?" The server smiled and waved off his politeness.

"No worries, honey. It's Evelyn."

"Mike." He shook her hand and realized he had no idea why he'd said "Mike."

She offered some parting reassurance before shuffling off to another customer. "Don't worry–you'll find him. When people get to that beach they fall in love with it all. The ocean, the horses... the whole nine yards. They'd give up their right arm to just stay there, planted in the sand, and not return to the insanity of the real world."

*   *   *

As Michael wove his way around the square pillars that propped up the ancient ceiling and led back to the front entrance (and exit) of BOB's, a man with red hair and dark sunglasses stepped in front of him. Lost in thought, Michael tried to skirt the gentleman, but quickly realized this person was intentionally blocking his route. When Michael looked up, he saw that the figure was in uniform, and a thought occurred to him: this person is from the Sheriff's office. Erica talked to someone, and whoever this is has information about Tom.

"The name's Nevelle. Herman Nevelle."

Despite the fact that the interior light of BOB's was exceptionally dim, Mr. Nevelle refused to remove his sunglasses.

Michael eyed him cautiously. "You with the Sheriff's office?"

Nevelle straightened his posture and sniffed. "I'm a Ranger for the Cape Lookout National Seashore. I keep an eye on Shackleford; patrol it daily to make sure visitors aren't tearing the place apart."

"Did you speak to Erica?"

"The Sheriff's office directed her to me. Yes, we talked." Nevelle pulled a chair out from the nearest table and motioned for Tom to join him.

"I haven't seen your friend." Nevelle removed his sunglasses, though Michael was still unable to get a good look at the man's face. "But I did find something."

Michael hadn't noticed that the man had a small bag slung over one shoulder, and he watched with a sense of trepidation as Nevelle fished out what appeared to be a lumpy object. After a few seconds, the Ranger placed a well-worn Nike running shoe on the table.

"That's his. That's Tom's."

Michael picked up the left shoe, which still held sand along the inside of the heel, and examined it as if it were an artifact from a bygone age.

"Is this all you have? What does this mean?" His breathing became more rapid, and a feeling he'd only experienced once before caused his mouth to run dry. He thought about that afternoon years ago, when he was zipping along Monroe Road, late for work, and clipped the leg of a teenager who tried to beat the red, blinking hand on the crosswalk signal that warned pedestrians to stop. The kid was alright after some superficial medical attention was administered by two exhausted-looking paramedics, but Michael somehow knew Tom's situation was much more dire.

Tom loved those shoes; they were lime green with orange "checks" flanking each side. They always provided an easy way to spot Tom in a crowd.

"I didn't find anything else. The shoe was sole-side up and wedged into a dune. A family that was sunbathing dumped their empty Diet Coke cans nearby, so I checked the area to be sure they hadn't left anything else, and, well... I found this. I've already contacted the Beaufort Police. Really, though, this doesn't mean anything. Maybe your friend had two pairs of shoes, and this fell out of his pack without him knowing. He could've already hopped the ferry and headed home. Maybe he's there now."

His car. Of course. "I'm an idiot," Michael barked with a deep exhale before turning to Nevelle.

"He drives a black Honda Civic. 2008. He would have parked it near the ferry dock. Can you take me there?"

When Nevelle stood, Michael could finally see the man's face and was momentarily jarred by the realization that the Ranger had only one eye. Where the other eye should have been was only a hole, and traversing the flesh above and below the socket was a deep scar. "Damn it, don't stare," Michael reminded himself. He averted his gaze and turned toward the door.

Behind him, Nevelle donned his sunglasses, sighed, and said, "Come on. We'll check it out together."

Chapter 3

The small gravel lot next to the ferry launch was illuminated by a single yellow bulb that barely clung to life. The thin light flickered periodically, reached full brightness, then wavered.

There were three cars in the lot: a silver Tahoe with South Carolina plates, a battered VW Beetle the color of mud, and there, in a far corner that was partially overgrown with ivy, a black Honda Civic. Michael slowly made his way to the car, waiting for the light overhead to complete its cycle. As if someone had flipped the switch on a spotlight, he suddenly saw the various decals—some peeling from the glass due to age and sun exposure—that were the tell-tale signs that this was, in fact, Tom's vehicle.

"That's it," Michael muttered, a defeated tone slumping his body into something akin to a wilted plant. He pointed to the Civic, and Nevelle's boots crunched across the loose rocks as he approached. He pulled a phone from his pocket and snapped a picture of the license plate.

"Erica, wasn't it? Do you want me to call her, or do you want to handle that? I'm going to file a report. In the morning, we'll take the ferry to the island." Nevelle adjusted his sunglasses and seemed to look down an alley on the other side of the empty street.

"I'll do it," Michael said. Nothing was certain at this point—it was still possible that Tom was alive, somewhere on that beach, being an incredible asshole. None of this tracked, though, and something instinctual told Michael that his friend was in the worst trouble of his life.

*　　　*　　　*

When the call ended, Michael placed his phone screen-side down on the nightstand next to the bed. He could hear the panic in Erica's voice, and he did everything he could to reassure her that Tom was probably fine; that they would almost certainly have more answers the next morning. He didn't really believe that, though–especially the part about Tom being okay. Everything that made Michael human told him that something sinister had occurred, and that whatever he was about to learn over the course of the next day or so was something that he'd never be able to fully shake.

It was 1:05 AM, and, as worried as he was, there wasn't anything else he could do that evening. The evidence was there: Tom was still in the area, and probably still on Shackleford. Michael wouldn't be able to get there until the first ferry departed at 8:30 AM. His bones ached, and he collapsed onto the comforter that the AirBnB host had smoothed into a perfect rectangle across the length of the bed.

When he switched off the bedside lamp, Michael surrendered to an exhaustion he hadn't known in years.

* * *

The blaring alarm from Michael's iPhone jolted him awake at 7:30 that morning. It was a clear day, and the sun beamed through the thin veil of curtain that faced the same street where BOB's was situated just thirty feet away. Michael checked his messages; there was a single text from Erica, asking if there had been any updates. This was followed by a plea to check in as soon as he learned something (which, of course, he would). After a quick shower, Michael was ready to venture out into the June humidity that coated eastern North Carolina like wet insulation.

When he stepped through the screen door that led away from his rental, Nevelle was there, wearing a freshly pressed shirt and the same sunglasses from the night before. He also had two steaming cups of coffee and blueberry muffins.

"How'd you sleep?"

"Much better than I expected," Michael replied, accepting the coffee with a nod of gratitude. "How much do I owe you?"

"Forget it." The Ranger waved a dismissive hand and looked toward the pier entrance about a quarter mile down the road. "Come on. Let's get moving. We can eat and talk."

The pair walked at a steady pace, sipping coffee and taking bites in between the bleating horns of sea vessels departing along the shoreline.

"Listen," Nevelle began. "I'm not sure what we're going to find when we get over there. The Sheriff is sending a Deputy, a guy named Clint, to tag along. They're convinced it hasn't been long enough to submit a report. Technically, forty-eight hours has to pass before an official missing persons situation can be filed. There hasn't been a true sign of a struggle, foul play, or anything like that. But, at my request, he agreed to at least send over one of his grunts."

Michael chewed on a large chunk of muffin silently and downed a heavy–and way too hot–gulp of coffee before chiming in.

"So, what's the plan, then? We'll go over there and just keep looking? Maybe start where you found the shoe?"

"Yeah, that's about it." Nevelle wiped his forehead with a napkin and drew in a deep breath. "There's something you should know."

Just as it seemed Nevelle was about to unspool some fact or observation that was way more ominous than anything Michael would have expected, a gentleman in beige law enforcement garb appeared from a storefront close to the ferry landing. The man had his own cup of coffee—twice as tall as theirs—and immediately derailed the conversation.

"Nevelle? Damn, man. Haven't seen you in ages."

The two men shook hands. "Good to see you, Clint. You've... uh... grown since the last time I saw you." Nevelle chuckled and turned his gaze toward Clint's gut (which, admittedly, looked as perfectly round and symmetrical as a basketball).

"Jesus. What kind of greeting is that?" Clint laughed and turned to Michael. "You must be Mike." Michael grimaced at the nickname. "Evelyn, the bartender at BOB's, told me you made it to town last night."

"Good to meet you. It's Michael. Mike is just an old nickname." Clint screwed his face a bit, finally settling on a wry smile. "I completely understand. I'm Clint Huffman. It used to be Clinton, but, well... it's a long story." Michael smiled for the first time in a couple of days. These guys were taking him seriously, and, in a world where it seemed like authenticity was in short supply, he felt like this stroke of luck was a good sign. Maybe this whole thing would have a positive outcome after all.

The three men walked the short distance to the ferry, which had already started boarding the line of customers that milled around the barnacled pylons. Down the street was the Seafarer Museum, a squat building covered in gray shingles with a giant anchor and ship wheel at the entrance. It was a fair distance away, maybe a hundred yards, but the outline of the anchor was distinct. He assumed this helped tourists find the place.

"I'm a part-time tour guide at the museum," Nevelle chimed in, noticing Michael's interest. "I'm usually there every other weekend. I love all things pirates. The history, the lore; I always found it fascinating."

Clint laughed. "Yeah. This fella's a Blackbeard freak. He'll tell you anything you want to know."

When the trio reached the landing, they paid their fare, boarded the boat, and settled into the plastic benches lining the rail.

"Don't you all have your own vessel for something like this?" If needed, Michael hoped they could get to the island more quickly (and stay there longer) than the ferry schedule would allow.

"Well, yeah, but another officer has it today. If this was a true missing person case," he paused, realizing the insensitivity of the comment. "Not that it isn't. Sorry. But, you know, the law—we have to wait before we can use the boat for something like that. I'm lucky I got the green light to pursue this today at all."

The engine roared to life, and the throttle shook the ferry from stem to stern.

"The Park Service has their own boat, and I usually have the full run of it. But there's a leak in one of the hydraulic lifts for the engine. I've had to take the ferry—on a taxpayer dime, of course—the past week because of that shit."

Nevelle and Clint exchanged laughs. Michael watched as the boat pushed away from the dock and slid into the channel leading to Shackleford. Other boats—some startlingly large, others ten feet at most—moved through the waterway on opposite sides of the triangular markers that led toward their destination.

It was clear these two men were seasoned in their respective fields, but there was something about Nevelle that struck Michael as odd. He seemed like an authentic person, but the eagerness with which Nevelle wanted to tell Michael whatever secret he harbored was unnerving. As soon as the Deputy had approached, Nevelle's whole demeanor changed.

People do this all the time, of course; especially if they're badmouthing a person and that same individual shows up out of the blue. "That Tina, she's a real... Oh, hey! Tina! We were just talking about you!"

That sort of thing.

This felt different. There was something the man was hiding, and that spooked Michael. What could he do, though? Who was he to refuse their aid? In the end, he just cared about his friend, and if these two could figure out what the hell was going on, then he didn't much care about their peculiarities.

The screech of seagulls circling overhead shook Michael from his reverie. The ferry was already arriving at the island, and the other visitors stood and began to group together at the bench where the three men had situated themselves for the short transit. Cell phones were removed from pockets and pictures were taken. Selfies seemed to be the preferred approach for the occasion. Michael was sure that someone was streaming the experience, or perhaps curating a taupe-colored reel that would show up on Instagram a few minutes later.

"Damn," he heard a young woman sneer. "The signal's gone."

"I guess Snapchat will have to wait," Michael thought with satisfaction. The comment reminded him that there was still a possibility that Tom had gotten a little too adventurous and lost his phone in the process. Or, if he'd managed to hang on to it, the signal was likely so weak that he couldn't call anyone. Either way, Tom's cell phone would be useless by now without a recharge.

The heavy ramp lowered from the ferry and connected with a concrete platform. The water here was gentle; it lapped against the vertical slab the vessel had approached, and dark green sea flora hugged the posts jutting from the waterline.

"All right, folks. End of the line. Have a great time and remember to keep your distance from the horses. They're used to people, but they're wild, and you just never know."

Clint and Nevelle chatted briefly with the Captain—a person that was, of course, local—and let him know that they might have to call in for an early evening pickup. The man pinched the length of gray beard at his chin with one hand as they spoke. When the exchange concluded, the Captain nodded, shook hands, and pulled back the grated ramp.

"Just use the landline when you're ready." The Captain pointed to a blue box perched on a rusted piece of aluminum at the end of the dock.

Was this really the only way to contact the town in the event of an emergency? A lean-to was positioned over the phone booth, and it looked like a structure that had just barely survived a wide variety of tropical storms and hurricanes.

Nevelle stretched as the boat churned away from the landing. He turned to Michael and Clint, the undulating surface of the Beaufort Channel reflecting in his aviators.

"Well, gentlemen, let's see what we can figure out. The dunes where I found the shoe are about two hundred yards that way, just around the point." Nevelle turned toward a long curvature in the shoreline. "We better get to it."

Chapter 4

By the time they reached the place where the Nike had been found, the sun was almost directly overhead. The morning air in town had been cool, but here, having just rounded the place on the island where they faced the open expanse of the Atlantic, things were strangely stagnant. Usually, a reliable gust would have provided a measure of relief for those setting up for picnics or surf fishing, but the air was still.

Nevelle guided the men to the spot where he had retrieved the shoe, at the base of several uneven dunes, beyond which were gently sloping hills of brush and coarse foliage. If Tom had been here and was feeling squirrely, Michael thought there was a decent chance that he would have set out to explore the area off the beaten path (where most visitors knew not to go).

"The shoe was here." The Ranger toed a depression in the sand with one boot. "There was nothing else, though." The men were all wearing sunglasses, but they still had to cup a hand over their brows to clearly get a sense of the surrounding terrain. The sun was intense and unobstructed.

"Mike–er, Michael..." Nevelle corrected himself quickly. "Why don't you check there, near the embankment. Like I said, I didn't find anything when I poked around the first time, but maybe the tide or the wind shook something loose."

Michael flicked a quick thumbs up and headed away from the men. When he looked over his shoulder, he saw Clint and Nevelle move away from one another in opposite directions, each with their heads down, presumably scanning the shoreline for anything that seemed out of place.

At the spot where the dunes flattened into open beach, Michael stopped. He knelt and slowly moved one hand through the loose grains. Other than the bone-dry claw of a long dead crab, he found nothing that raised any flags. He stood, the enormity of the location and situation shaking his faith that anything definitive might emerge from this search. Just as he was about to move toward Nevelle (who was already a faint figure in the midmorning haze), Michael heard a high-pitched squeal.

He climbed one of the stout dunes and there, just visible amid the brush, he saw a wing. Its feathers were contrasting shades of snow and ash, and the wing flapped several times. Then, another wing became visible, several feet away, rising above the green-gray line of scant greenery peppering the landscape.

Michael slowly made his way toward what he presumed were a couple of seagulls. As he approached, an additional pair of wings rose above the scrub. Several more paces brought him to the scene.

Knees buckling, Michael fell to the thorny surface. His vision momentarily blurred. There, gleaming in the unobstructed sun, was an arm. A human arm. When one thinks about a scenario like this, the tendency is to think of a movie; a prop, crafted in a practical effects workshop, clearly fake and drenched in red corn syrup. He knew that what he gawked at was real; chunks had been removed in what looked like large, crescent-shaped bites. At one juncture of the maimed limb Michael could see the ulna (or maybe it was the radius?), a length of yellowish-white bone that appeared to have been scraped roughly. The hand was still attached, though several fingers were missing. It was an oddly bloodless sight, and the seagulls that loudly defended their find flapped and trotted in a wide circle.

Suddenly filled with a potent mix of profound sorrow and uninhibited rage, Michael stood and chased away the birds. They took to the air in all directions, screeching wildly. The commotion drew the attention of Nevelle and Clint, who were running as fast their middle-aged forms would allow.

When they reached Michael, they found him seated by what remained of the extremity.

"Oh, Christ." Clint backed away from the grisly sight with one hand over his mouth. After collecting himself, the Deputy checked his cell phone and turned to Nevelle. "I don't have a signal. I've gotta go to the payphone. Herman, don't let any other visitors come over here. Tape it off somehow. We have to get the other officers to the island. Now."

As Clint sprinted back in the direction they'd come from, Nevelle lowered himself so that he was facing Michael.

"Are you sure it's him?"

Michael looked away from Nevelle, pointing a shaky finger at the wrist that was half concealed by a winding tendril interspersed with sand spurs. There, Nevelle saw a watch, still clasped to its owner, displaying the time and date.

"That Casio G-Shock... It was a joke between us. I got it for him on his fortieth birthday."

Nevelle put a hand on Michael's shoulder.

"I'm so sorry." He stood and took stock of how many tourists were nearby. An elderly couple shuffled along the shoreline, but Michael and the Ranger were otherwise alone.

"I have to tape this off. It's a crime scene now. The calvary will be here soon." Nevelle produced a roll of yellow tape from his backpack. "Think you could help me?"

23

Standing, Michael nodded quietly and walked away from Nevelle in order to wrap the tape around a gathering of cattails that were close by.

Once they had sectioned off a tiny square of the island, Nevelle removed his sunglasses and looked directly at Michael. The man's one remaining eye didn't lose its focus when he spoke.

"Before they get here, I need you to listen to what I have to say."

Chapter 5

"You're not the first Michael I've ever met."

Michael stared at Nevelle. "Well, yeah," he thought. "Michael was the most common boy name in 1982, the year I was born." He didn't say any of this. Instead, he just looked directly at the one-eyed Ranger, wondering where this monologue could possibly be going.

"It was 2009, late March. I was a Park Ranger in the Uwharrie National Forest. You heard of it?"

Michael was indeed familiar with the vast stretch of wilderness. When a person drove east from Charlotte on Highway 73, they'd eventually run into the town of Albemarle. There wasn't much to it; a few crossroads, some highway intersections, and just enough fast food restaurants to provide the illusion of variety. From there, Highway 27 snaked through dense woodland toward the town of Troy, which was smack dab in the middle of the Uwharrie National Forest.

Wait: Troy? He'd heard about that place at some point. Something happened there; something notable enough to make the national news. But that was a long time ago.

"Anyway, I was on patrol one night. The whole area is pretty lowkey. There are people passing through all the time, but it's one of those places mostly populated with locals; people whose great, great grandparents had lived there. That kind of thing."

Nevelle massaged the pink scar that climbed over his eyebrow and away from the empty socket.

"There was an abandoned farm outside of Troy. Two young guys from Charlotte had made their way onto the property to do some camping one weekend. They weren't well-prepared; they had canned food and other items, like a tent and some things to build a fire. I had been circling the edge of the forest for an hour when I heard the screams."

The Ranger looked toward the beach to check on the couple he'd seen meandering just minutes before. They had continued down the shore, seemingly unaware of the taped off area just over the dune ridge.

"When I finally made it to them, the scene was pure chaos. Before I knew what was going on something grabbed me. Something big." Nevelle bit his lip and pointed to the place where his eye had been. "It did this. It was..." He breathed in deeply, as if he'd told this story too many times before and received a reaction that had completely worn him down. "It was Bigfoot."

Michael felt an anger rising inside of him. Was this guy serious? Bigfoot? His friend was missing and, based on the now severed arm that had been discovered, very likely dead. And this Park Ranger wanted to talk about Bigfoot?

"What? What the hell are you talking about?"

Nevelle manufactured a weak smile. "I know. You don't think I've gotten this reaction before? You remember the news story, don't you? The bodies they found in the forest?"

It had been fourteen years, but he was beginning to remember. A fog was lifting from somewhere in his memory, and the horrific details reemerged. Young men had been found in the woods, all of them dismembered. There was no rhyme or reason to the slaughter. Local police, the SBI, and the FBI all coordinated for three weeks, but, other than some hair samples that were ultimately attributed to a black bear, the case was inconclusive.

"Yeah, I remember." Michael was supremely annoyed, and he was waiting for Nevelle to make a relevant connection. "What does that have to do with Shackleford Island?"

"The unsubstantiated conclusion by most 'experts' was that a rabid bear had killed the hikers. The coroner determined that was the most likely cause, and there was tremendous pressure to provide some kind of answer. When no clear human suspect could be identified, well, the bear story is where the whole thing landed. Everyone wanted it over and done with."

Nevelle pulled a tall, plastic bottle filled with water from his pack. He unscrewed the cap and let it hang by its plastic ring before taking three prolonged gulps.

"Anyway, I couldn't let it go. When the dust settled and I was back on patrol, I quietly did my own research. I started interviewing people. No one wanted to say anything, but there was a pattern. In the years preceding the incident, the folks who lived near the forest heard strange noises. Almost like a deep whoop that turned into–and I'm using their words–a 'grotesque howl.' Closer into town people said it was a regular thing. People dismissed it as some kind of bird mating call or a demented coyote."

The Ranger led Michael away from the slowly rotting arm. It was just as well; he had a hard time not looking at it. The watch still snugly secured around the wrist felt like a grim beacon that, with the cycling of each digital number, some kind of unseen horror on the island drew nearer to them.

"Then peoples' pets started vanishing. A dachshund here, a tabby cat there. This happened over the course of months, but because the place is so rural, people didn't think much of it. Animals run off. It happens, especially when your backyard is an untouched forest."

The sun was directly overhead and had already started its crawl toward the western sky. Michael turned to the landing and could see that the ferry had returned; a cacophony of local cops and people in various uniforms rounded the point and marched in their direction.

Nevelle saw the throng moving along the beach and hurried his story. "The sounds eventually vanished, but I kept an ear to the ground. And guess what? Reports started popping up of similar occurrences in Aberdeen, thirty-five miles away. Then Hope Mills. And the slate of disappearing dogs and late-night whoops kept moving east until it ended here, just outside of Beaufort."

The long procession of police and volunteer firefighters—what were firefighters doing here?—was nearing them, and Nevelle kicked his story into high gear.

"I requested relocation to the Cape Lookout National Seashore. I've been here for two years, and the occurrences have been few and far between. But that arm—listen, I'm telling you. I know this is hard to hear. But I'm telling you, that tear at the end of it... where it met the shoulder. It wasn't a cut. It was a rip. And it exactly matches what I saw in the Uwharrie. This is the first real evidence I've seen that—somehow—that beast managed to isolate himself here."

"Herman Nevelle?" A Beaufort Police officer he didn't know approached with one hand extended. Nevelle took it and waited for the man to introduce himself. "Bert Marshburn. We got the report. What can we do?"

The line of public servants had come to a standstill, all listening carefully and eyeing the taped off area just a few feet away.

"Fan out and document every inch of this island. Whatever–er, whoever–did this is still here. I'm sure of it."

"How do you know?" Bert was sweating and had one hand perched on the revolver dangling from his waist.

"Call it a hunch. If nothing else, with a party like this we'll probably find more evidence. Something that can really nail the bastard."

Bert smiled and nodded, then looked grimly at the nearby arm. "You heard him. Split into groups of four. Report back here in one hour." The officer tightened his lips and motioned for a subordinate to join him. "Bill: bag that. It's evidence. Get Ted over here, and make sure he has his camera."

Nevelle turned his gaze to Michael and pointed to a herd of wild horses that were stamping at the brush closer to the center of the island.

"Come on. We're going that way."

Chapter 6

The unlikely pair continued talking as they approached the horses, all of which seemed wholly unaffected by their presence. A few of the mares raised their heads from where they grazed and studied them with vague curiosity. Ears twitching, they eventually returned to the thick vegetation.

"These horses are opportunists." Nevelle slowly approached the herd, which, they learned, was only so tolerant of the two men encroaching on their territory. After a brown horse with white spots reared and whinnied loudly, the cluster took off, moving deeper into the island, toward a dark line of trees that closed in around the horizon. There was a wildness here that Michael hadn't anticipated, and he wondered how much deeper into the interior they would need to go.

The Ranger moved in on where the horses had been gathered to see if anything of interest stood out on the landscape. He moved in a slow shuffle, overturning a gnarled log here and shell-laden rock there. Eventually he stopped, peering down at something that wasn't immediately visible to Michael.

"I'll be damned." He knelt, fished around in the sand, and finally stood. He held a green running shoe in his right hand. "From the other foot."

Michael approached to examine the other Nike, and saw that it had small, flat spots of dried blood along the toe. Nevelle saw this too and turned his attention back to the dirt. Just past the brush line they saw the same maroon circles, tiny and constellation-like, dotting the dry soil and clearly moving away from where they stood. They began walking without saying a word, following the trail as best they could. In places it disappeared and then just as quickly reappeared, the spots sometimes larger and more pronounced on a broad leaf or bleached tree limb. It wasn't long before they stood at the edge of a surprisingly dense forest.

"Live oak, red cedar, and American holly. They're all intertwined here. Incredibly dense and notoriously tough to navigate."

Nevelle once again flipped his backpack around, this time extracting a sheathed machete. It wasn't overly large, but when the Ranger removed the blade's covering, Michael realized that the tool was well-maintained and exceedingly sharp.

"Shouldn't we tell the others?"

Michael suddenly felt a tinge of hesitation about venturing into this coastal forest. His best guess was that, at its maximum, the trees were thirty feet tall. He could already tell, though, that this was going to be a monumental slog. He felt like they were moving a little too quickly here, and, to his shame, Michael was, for the first time on this trip, more concerned for his own well-being than that of his missing friend.

"I've done a lot of research. Everything I've found suggests that these creatures are mostly nocturnal. By the time we backtrack and round up a crew, well, we might lose our chance."

"Lose our chance for what?" In that moment, Michael perceived something in Nevelle; a primal, almost obsessive need to accomplish something now–that very instant.

"I know I sounded crazy back there. Really, I do. I've had people look at me like that ever since that sasquatch tried to kill me. But you have to trust me." He stretched out one arm and angled the machete toward what looked like impenetrable forest. "There is a beast in there. A real, honest-to-God monster. It killed your friend, and it will kill again if we don't do something. Please."

Nevelle wasn't done with his backpack. Plunging in an arm he quickly returned with a small pistol, still in its leather holster. Michael was shocked. He'd been to a firing range once in his life with a group of friends, and the recoil of those few shots had scared the shit out of him.

"You ever used one of these?"

Michael nodded reluctantly. "Yeah. At a range, a long time ago. Like... a really long time ago."

"There's nothing to it." Nevelle was serious before, but his demeanor suddenly acquired a whole new level of listen-to-me-and-don't-look-away severity.

"This is the safety." He thumbed a small switch on the side of the weapon, and then repeated the process. "Keep it on until I tell you to flip the switch. I mean that. Do not mess with this until I give the word."

Michael was petrified. He hated firearms. In the end, though, he hated the thought of returning to Charlotte and telling Erica that, at the last second, he chickened out because there were some trees on a beach that he simply refused to check out.

"Okay. Not until you say."

"Good man." Nevelle returned the empty machete sheath to his backpack. "You've got seven shots with that. You just aim–line up the sight with where you want the bullets to go; hold the gun straight–and wait 'til the target is close. You won't miss."

Michael hadn't brought a bag of any type, so he stuffed the gun–holster and all–in the back of his shorts, because, well, isn't that what people do? He didn't have much choice, he realized, but he also knew there was a decently solid chance that he'd end up shooting his ass off.

"Come on. Let's get to it."

Nevelle led the way, and with a heavy swing of his machete, the two men began their descent into hell.

*   *   *

There was a rhythm to Nevelle's chopping that seemed to blend with the distant booming of the surf. That morning a red flag had been raised, causing the presence of swimmers on the beaches of Shackleford to be minimal. A few small boats bobbed in the surf along the narrow strip of beach, but, for such a beautiful day in a prime summer month, things were oddly still and quiet.

The further they ventured into the trees, the clearer it became that the machete was only going to get the job done for so long. A chainsaw would be needed to make any real progress among the thick brambles.

The sun managed to penetrate here and there, and, at intervals, the dry blood spatter continued to act as a gruesome signpost. They stepped forward, muttering and pointing to help one another work around some impenetrable bit of grove. Nevelle and Michael continued in this manner for the better part of two and a half hours, the ever-faithful blood trail keeping them on track.

Michael came to the realization that the sheer amount of blood they encountered as they ventured forward was a dire omen. There's no way Tom had survived whatever happened to him; he'd have lost pints by the time any help arrived.

He studied Nevelle as they winced and cursed in an effort to continue onward. The Ranger seemed certain that a bigfoot (Was this the Bigfoot?), or some kind of hereto undiscovered cryptid, was responsible for the mayhem that now engulfed the island. A reclusive axe murderer seemed like a much more logical likelihood. Still, Nevelle seemed one hundred percent committed to the idea that something supernaturally strong had done this to Tom. Michael couldn't yet buy into that theory, but as he felt the weight of the gun tucked into the rear of his shorts jostle with every uncertain step, he couldn't shake the notion that something dark was waiting for them.

Suddenly, the sun seemed to have completely faded from existence. The branches and foliage had coiled in upon one another with such determination and thickness that a muted, ambient light was the only thing that allowed them to see two feet in front of them.

Nevelle raised a hand. He then placed a finger over his lips, signaling for Michael to eliminate all unnecessary noise. In the ever-increasing darkness they heard a heavy breathing that was not their own.

Nevelle flattened his right hand, moving it slowly up and down, telling Michael that they were proceeding forward. The pair reached a thicket that looked like a wall of leaves. The foliage was slightly discolored, and it looked like it was composed of mostly dead branches that had been primitively woven together. They were dry and would rattle if disturbed, but Nevelle somehow managed to separate a section with such silence and care that Michael was tempted to snap his fingers next to his own ears to make sure he hadn't gone deaf.

Nevelle's efforts created a two-foot-wide hole that allowed the men to look into an opening. Faint sunlight illuminated the center of the den they craned to see, and suddenly it hit them: the stench of something dead. It was overwhelming and almost caused Nevelle to gag. Covering his mouth and pinching his nose, Michael leaned forward. He was awestruck by the scene.

Tom was there—well, most of Tom. His torso remained, though the arms and legs had been removed. He looked like some kind of Halloween prop you'd see on a front lawn in a middle-class neighborhood, put there by an overzealous dad that was trying extra hard to gross out the kids down the street. Flies buzzed loudly. Tom's face was frozen in horror, his eyes wide, and a surprised expression twisted his mouth. Blood caked the places where his extremities had been removed, and Michael caught sight of a leg, bent unnaturally at the knee, resting in one corner of the twelve-foot-wide space.

Nevelle held his nose and motioned with one hand.

They had found the creature.

Michael stared in disbelief, his brain working overtime to make sense of what he saw. Despite his best efforts to rationalize what the beast could really be (the result of some failed military experiment, perhaps?), something told Michael that Nevelle had been telling him the truth.

This was a sasquatch. They were real.

The creature snored loudly, its great chest draped in thick, brown hair rising and falling with the now barely audible breakers. The animal's face was turned away from them, but they could see the remains of Tom's other arm by the monster's side. It had picked the thing clean; what remained looked like the result of someone trying to consume every last morsel of a chicken wing, leaving only the gristle and sinewy bits.

Michael hadn't even realized that tears were streaming down his face. He was squeezing a hand tight against his mouth, doing everything he could to contain the scream that was building in his throat. The Ranger eagerly gestured for Michael to take a deep breath; to calm down and regain focus. Nevelle also displayed a wide, open palm, motioning to the pistol that protruded from under Michael's shirt.

Inhaling deeply, Michael reached for the gun. He closed his fingers around the smooth leather that contained the weapon and pulled the bundle from his waist, handing it to Nevelle as quietly as possible. The Ranger stared at the brass clasp that buttoned the gun into the holster. Even in the growing dark of the woods, Michael could see the sweat beading along Nevelle's hand as he worked to free the gun from the holster. Amazingly, the button came loose with an almost inaudible click. Michael imagined the sound had been lost in the breeze that shook the treetops overhead, but he couldn't be sure. Thumbing the safety into the "OFF" position, Nevelle turned back to the hole that led into the creature's lair.

The two of them had been so focused on the pistol that they didn't realize the animal was now standing in the middle of the den, its full height revealed. A low, prehistoric grumble shook the black leaves surrounding them.

"Shit."

Nevelle drew a sharp breath, spun on one heel, and fired.

Chapter 7

The report from the handgun echoed across the small island. Clint stood abruptly and watched as a flock of birds rose above the heart of the forest that concealed the geographic center of Shackleford. He pulled a radio from his hip and waited for the crackle of static to subside.

"This is Huffman. Shots fired. Or, actually, a shot." He trailed off and realized the time. The sun had become a wavering disc of orange that danced over the sea. Purple and pink hues spread to either end of the horizon, and Clint knew it wouldn't be long before night overtook them.

"I heard it." Another officer somewhere on the island replied. "Where's Herman?"

Clint didn't think much of it when Nevelle and the visitor from Charlotte didn't check in at the designated rendezvous. A lot of the guys who had volunteered for the manhunt had taken a wrong turn and been sidetracked by false leads and bits of trash. Most of them had just made their way back to Huffman in the past twenty minutes.

"Damned if I know. But there are only a handful of folks who haven't returned, and he's one of them." Clint rubbed his chin and nodded quickly. "Get back here as soon as you can and send someone to call the ferry. I have a feeling we're going to need more bodies on this one."

*   *   *

The bullet was true to its mark, striking the beast in its left shoulder. Nevelle had intended to deliver a fatal wound to its matted forehead, but the speed with which he had pulled the trigger caused him to overcorrect his aim.

An agonized howl exploded from the creature, and Michael was stunned by the ferocity and swiftness with which it moved. It was borderline mesmerizing. The sasquatch was momentarily held back by its own creation, the tightly assembled wall that separated its den from the rest of the forest. The monster wrestled with the branches for only a few moments before breaking through, at which point both Nevelle and Michael had been racing in the opposite direction for a solid ten seconds.

The two didn't speak; they only breathed and moved, pumping their arms and winding through the bramble with a precision that had inexplicably been missing over the course of the past several hours. Michael discovered that imminent death is a shockingly effective motivator.

Behind them, the beast closed the distance with terrifying speed. It didn't have to worry about navigating the never-ending branches; it simply splintered any obstructions as it barreled forward, a spectacle of brute force. The sasquatch was a juggernaut of muscle and hair that was hellbent on killing these intruders.

A yelp pierced the jungle and caused Michael to stop, his heels slicing through the sandy soil as he skidded to a standstill. He saw Nevelle, the Ranger's one eye wide with terror, being lifted from the ground by his neck. The bigfoot's hand was absolutely gigantic, and it held the Ranger in the air as if he were a cheap lamp that was about to be broken into clean segments so that it could be stuffed into a trashcan. Then something caught Michael's eye.

As the beast slowly rotated Nevelle toward him so they could look one another in the face, the blade of the machete the Ranger carried glinted in the soft light that still managed to penetrate the vegetation overhead.

The smell of the monster was nauseating. The sasquatch pulled Nevelle closer so that he could inspect his prey. When the creature saw the single eye that returned his gaze, a flash of recollection seemed to spill across its face. It knew this human.

The sasquatch bared its teeth, several incisors primed and ready to puncture as deeply as they were able. The fangs were a sickly yellow, bits of food–bits of Tom?–stuck to the gumline. Just as the bigfoot opened its maw, it squawked in pain and tossed Nevelle to the ground. The creature turned to find a machete buried in its right thigh, and a line of blood slowly running down its knee and ankle, pooling atop the cold ground cover of the forest floor. Michael backed away from the point of the strike, a chill running through him.

The beast gripped the machete and plucked it from his leg. Nevelle was already up, steadying himself against the now slightly less dense brush, reflexively clutching at his neck in an effort to catch his breath. The gash was deep, and the animal placed both hands around its leg and stumbled back into the darkness. The men kept their eyes locked on the monster; its pupils reflected what little light there was, like a deer on a country road that had been surprised by an unexpected pair of high beams.

"Back away. Slowly. Just keep staring." His breathing was halting and labored, but Nevelle was moving, and he motioned for Michael to continue slowly making his way toward the beach. Soon, the monster was absorbed by the interior of the wilderness, and the two men had quickened their pace–insomuch as the lessening thickets would allow–until they were awarded with a full view of the setting sun.

When they finally escaped the woods, Clint had just arrived, panting heavily, both hands on his knees.

"What the hell was that? Y'all okay?"

Nevelle's neck was covered in five dark bruises, but that appeared to be the extent of the damage.

"Far from it, friend." The three of them continued to back away from the wood line, even as the gathering troupe of volunteers and law enforcement officials clicked on flashlights and pointed them toward the stout forest, wondering what lay within the darkness.

Chapter 8

"Say what now?"

Clint sat on the beach next to Nevelle, his mouth hanging open as he tried to make sense of what he was being told. The others who had spent the day scouring the sand for clothing, shreds of tent, or anything that might lead to some kind of clarity about the missing camper stood in tight circles and murmured about what all of this might mean for tourist season and people's willingness to visit the island (and, by extension, Beaufort).

"I know, Clint. It sounds insane. But this guy will back me up." Nevelle turned to Michael, who realized he hadn't spoken with Erica since late the previous evening. As if reading his mind, Nevelle interrupted him. "I know. I'll call her. I still have her number. That conversation is something I'll handle." The weight of what that meant settled on Michael. Really, delivery of this type of news was a thing the local police should facilitate, but given the oddity of the circumstances, Clint simply snorted an agreement.

"Tell him what we saw." The Ranger stood uneasily and made his way toward the sole payphone on the island.

"Well?" Clint was quiet for a few moments, allowing Michael as much time as he needed to respond.

"We saw something."

"Something." Clint didn't like that answer. He was a man of specifics. "Give me the details."

"It was a... thing. A creature. It was covered in hair, maybe eight feet tall. It wasn't a bear or anything like that. It wasn't a horse. It was something else."

"I can't believe I'm asking this, but was it..." he paused and did what he could to stifle his growing annoyance. "...was it a bigfoot?" The Deputy shook his head and tried not to smile.

Michael shrugged. "Yes. No. Maybe? I don't know what else it could have been. It was bipedal, and it had hands. Really big hands. And it was pissed."

"So, our perp isn't a human, then. It's an animal."

Michael nodded, then continued.

"What kind of animal, though, I can't say. If ever I've seen a sasquatch in the flesh, well, that was it."

Huffman stood and surveyed the personnel he had available.

"I can't tell these fellas we're chasing Bigfoot. You understand me?" He looked around and seemed to be lost in thought. "I believe you saw something. It was probably a bear. I've seen those shows before. People get scared and always think a bear or some shit is actually a sasquatch."

The Deputy placed his hands on his hips, cleared his throat, and spoke as loudly as he could.

"Okay, everyone, listen up." People broke away from their conversations and filed around the small fire one of them had constructed on the beach. Night had fallen; the sun was gone, and a blue-black sky unfurled overhead.

"We might have a wild animal situation. Maybe a rabid black bear. I don't know for sure. Animal Control isn't going to be able to lug their gear across the channel, so the solution is simple: we're going to hunt this thing down. We're going to kill it. We're going to collect evidence so that the coroner can match the bite marks on the victim, and we're going to be sure that the public knows that a crazed murderer hasn't set up shop on Shackleford."

A lot of these guys were young and eager for a little adventure. They smiled and quietly joked with one another, unzipping black duffel bags and opening boxes of ammunition.

"But we're going to do this in an orderly, organized fashion. Danny, you take the lead on firearms. Only a handful of you are getting guns; the rest are going to help us track this thing." Though they tried to suppress it, many of them couldn't help but groan in disappointment.

"We are absolutely not going to shoot at anything until we have a clear line of sight and an idea of what the hell this thing really is." Clint was speaking more loudly now, doing everything he could to underscore the gravity of his point. "I will not stand for an unapproved discharge. If anyone fires without my greenlight, you're on the ferry and I'm contacting your supervisor first thing tomorrow. That's how it's gonna be. None of us are getting cut down by friendly fire."

The man who Michael assumed was Danny had already begun directing several of the men to group together near the fire for additional instructions.

Michael raised a hand, because he wasn't sure how else to cut through the intensity Clint had cast over the situation.

"Yes?" The Deputy looked at Michael and didn't hide his agitation.

"It's wounded. Nevelle shot it. I buried a machete in one of its legs."

Huffman raised an eyebrow. "Herman didn't mention that."

"It's hurt. The gunshot wound is in its shoulder, and the gash in its leg is deep. But it walked away. Given its size and speed..." Michael took a moment to look at everyone else on the beach, most of them now a series of shadows moving in the firelight. "...I don't think it's done. I think it's angry. And I think this is going to be a long night."

An aura of disbelief hung in the air, and Clint did what he could to bring the conversation back to something actionable. "Okay. It's wounded. Keep an eye out for blood and move in groups of five. Do not break off and try to be a hero."

By this time Nevelle had returned. He came to a large log that had been placed near the fire and collapsed onto it. Michael approached the Ranger and took a seat on the dusty piece of oak.

"She's inconsolable. Her dad is going to pick her up, and they're coming tomorrow morning." Nevelle shifted his weight and tried to stretch his legs. He was clearly sore from the torturous hike that ate up their afternoon. "So, what did Deputy Take-Charge have to say?"

Michael recounted the plan and general approach they had been ordered to follow. The Ranger listened intently. He checked his backpack and grunted a response of acknowledgement.

"Better now than later, but this isn't going to be easy. You saw its strength, and it's smarter than they know. People are going to die tonight, but if we play our cards right, we can end this."

Nevelle stood and Michael followed. The Deputy waved both arms and shouted, "It's time! Move out!"

With that, the hunt was on.

Chapter 9

The creature positioned himself at the center of his den. Because his eyes were accustomed to operating in the dark, he had no trouble finding the tools he needed. The animal ripped away a length of red nylon from the crumpled remnants of the tent that had provided Tom with his final hour of peaceful slumber. Picking up a clump of root-laden moss, the sasquatch forced it into the aching valley that had been carved into his leg. The thing moaned in a low, deep manner, and, as best he could, tied the fabric in overlapping layers around the ramshackle patch job. He fastened an especially stiff section of reed at the back of the knot and twisted it to secure the dressing. The beast's leg throbbed, but he knew the moss would soon quiet the wound.

The creature's shoulder injury didn't matter. His muscles were dense and wrapped around one another like thick copper wiring. As he healed, the bullet would naturally be pushed out of his body over the course of the following week.

Standing slowly, the sasquatch tested the makeshift bandage. It held, and he felt reasonably sure it would endure the sprinting and strain that it would surely encounter as the evening progressed. He made his way to a mat of dead twigs and pulled it aside. A long segment of horse bone had been concealed there, and he withdrew it from a small pit in the earth. The monster had used an especially sharp fragment of fossilized shell to sharpen one end to a point that would easily draw blood with the softest contact. He then swatted away the flies clinging to what remained of Tom's torso. The creature knew he would need fuel for what was to come. Gripping the bone tightly, he impaled the slumped torso, raised it to his face, and, stretching his jaws wide, tore a sizable chunk of meat away from the abdomen.

Though the animal had relied on berries and vegetation for the bulk of its life, the events that occurred in the woods all those years ago had awakened a taste for meat. The territorial violation those men were guilty of was something he couldn't forget. That was where it all started.

There were so few of his species left; he barely remembered his own kin, a small unit of three other sasquatches that lived quietly in the heart of the forest for decades. When the bigfoot stumbled upon the hikers that had crossed the border into their dominion, he knew he had to do something. When they wouldn't leave and he had concluded that direct engagement was the only real course of action, he hadn't expected that his animal instinct to use his teeth as a weapon would result in a persistent need for human flesh. He craved its taste; the way it cemented an all-consuming feeling of victory and dominance.

The war he waged on that small band of trespassers resulted in the arrival of even more of the intrusive beings, and the only other of his kind he had ever known disappeared into the wilderness. Though he had searched, something told him they were gone forever. That was their way. They were, at a certain point in life, given to existing as solitary creatures, only staying in one another's company long enough to reproduce. That was when he decided to claim new territory.

He left his home, and a cycle began. The intruders plagued his every attempt at peace, causing his anger to become deeper and more profound. At each location he attempted to settle, humans eventually arrived, and the very sight of their presence transformed him into a brute defined by rage. He saw only red as they trampled his newly staked enclave.

With each human transgression, his immediate recourse was to maim and slaughter.

The bigfoot didn't feel remorse, really. It eventually became a habitual inclination to survive and consume. There was something almost religious involved with killing and eating the very things that attempted to drive him out of his home. The inevitable slaughter was barbaric, but, in the end, completely and utterly satisfying. And, the creature surmised, tonight would be something ethereal and definitive. He had reached the end of the world and couldn't make sense of the limitless sea that closed him in on all sides. The sasquatch would make a stand here and eradicate as many of these humans as possible. There was nowhere else to go.

Using one of its massive feet to push the grotesque chunk of Tom from the horse bone and onto the floor of his den, the creature stretched and groaned. He could sense something in the air and knew the end of humans was near. Tightly gripping his weapon in both hands, the beast inhaled deeply and bellowed a primal roar. The monster then ripped away a section of his den wall, revealing the pitch-black undergrowth beyond. The animal lunged forward, his eyes glowing, and thundered into the night.

*   *   *

The men had spread to all corners of the island, but the majority were hesitant to journey into the wooded interior. When the last echoes of a deep and distant animal call made it to the edge of the beach, their blood ran cold. Most of the men stopped walking and stood as rigid as fence posts, a cold sweat enveloping them like morning dew. Flashlight beams floated in the darkness, and the various squads that had broken away to explore the island were unsure of how to proceed.

Clint had joined Michael and Nevelle, and the three men walked slowly, about five feet apart. The Deputy held the stock of a twelve-gauge, his hand slick with perspiration, barely able to level the flashlight that granted them a clear field of view some twenty feet ahead. Nevelle had wanted to give the handgun to Michael once again, but he knew that wouldn't fly with Clint. The Ranger gripped the weapon with both hands, its muzzle pointed toward the ground as they advanced. Michael had the machete, and he felt pretty good about that; after all, it had been exponentially more effective than he'd anticipated during his first encounter with the beast.

Barely perceptible dunes shaped the horizon, obscuring the ocean beyond. The men could see the far-off glow of flashlights.

"Clint, you're not going to want to hear this, but that shotgun is only going to slow it down. It won't do any real damage." Nevelle kept his one eye forward, but he could feel the stare coming from his friend. The Deputy's gut rose and fell noticeably, his breathing shallow. The man was clearly rattled.

"What the hell am I supposed to do, then?"

Nevelle shrugged. "Aim for his knees. The fact that Mike somehow cut it as deeply as he did... Well, that's something. It tells me there might actually be a weakness we can exploit. If we can immobilize it, even for a second..."

Ragged shrieks peeled across the windswept dunes. The men stopped and turned to one another. Clint peered into the darkness and saw lights blinking out one by one, a long way to the east.

"Shit."

The trio began to sprint toward the madness unfolding on the beach two hundred yards away.

Shackleford Banks Sasquatch

*   *   *

When the bigfoot exited the tree line, he encountered four humans. They didn't see him right away. Nearing the beach, the creature lightened his steps, taking special care not to break any large limbs that had fallen during the most recent storm. Momentum and silence were his allies. The bigfoot blended with the brush, hunched and ready to launch himself at the unsuspecting hunting party.

"Do you smell that?" The men paused for a moment, their artificial lights trained on the retreating tide, attempting to locate the source of the odor. With their attention averted, the sasquatch separated itself from the camouflage of the wilderness and rocketed into a sprint.

"Oh my God!" A single ray of light illuminated the beast's face, its eyes burning and an insatiable rage fueling its swiftness. The group was momentarily paralyzed by the realization that the man at their far left was being held aloft, the luminous moon providing a ghastly halo as he tried to free himself. The victim was so surprised by his situation that he looked around in confusion, trying to hash out how he had miraculously ascended to such a great height. When he realized that an impossibly large and coarse implement had been shoved directly through his stomach–and that an equally colossal ape-like being had raised him skyward, as if he were some kind of hideous flag–the man wailed in a way that his friends had not expected. Then, with a final wheeze and gasp, his head slumped forward.

Blood mixed with the sea foam that flicked in the breeze along the shore. The gargantuan beast swung the length of bone, and the limp body at its end ragdolled into the surf. Shaken from his stupor, one of the remaining three men fired a revolver. The shots were panicked and forced; the monster seemed to waltz through the scene, grabbing one of the men by a leg and, using his ever-increasing momentum, slamming the poor soul into the sand headfirst. A sickening crack was heard, and the main flailed in the sand.

Screaming with as much ferocity as he could muster, one of the two survivors charged the animal with a comically large bowie knife. The sasquatch dodged the first slash, then, clutching the wrist that held the knife, the monster twisted in a way that caused the man's hand to pop off like a bottlecap. A gush of warm blood spilled from the break, and the man stumbled back in shock.

Still holding the separated hand and the accompanying knife, the monster approached his stunned victim and buried the blade in the top of the human's head. A reactionary whimper tumbled from his lips, and the creature could see the glint of moonlight on the metal clearly visible in the man's open mouth. From behind, the bigfoot heard a rhythmic, mechanical sound; one he'd heard at various intervals over the course of his life.

Click. Click. Click.

The lone survivor had depleted his ammunition. The still shadowed bigfoot was breathing heavily, and as it turned toward the man who vainly searched his belt pouch for bullets, the insanity of the scene became evident. Pieces of his companions littered the otherwise seaweed-covered stretch of coastline. Blood had pooled in the erratic footsteps left in the sand. Seawater washed in, diluting the macabre mixture in the tide.

The sasquatch lumbered forward and crouched in order to face its quarry eye-to-eye. The man only blinked, unable to move. When he realized he was urinating, the human relented and dropped the gun by his side.

The beast picked up the man as one might a toddler, by the armpits and with surprising care. The monster waded into the water until he was waist-deep in the booming surf and lowered his victim into the saltwater. When the thrashing subsided, the sasquatch emerged from the ocean, retrieved his sharpened bone, and made his way toward the herd of feral horses perched on a sandy hillock.

*   *   *

By the time Nevelle and Michael reached the location of the terrified shouts it was too late. A single flashlight was still illuminated, its handle stuck vertically in the sand, creating an eerie spotlight that reached up and disappeared in the dark haze.

The Ranger stepped gingerly around the sight of the massacre, keeping his eyes trained on the nearby brush as he went. Nausea swept over Michael as it had earlier in the day at the sight of Tom's mangled remains. Mercifully, the single ray from the flashlight was pointed toward the stars and offered only a muted sense of the carnage strewn about them.

Michael did what he could to settle himself. "Should we move the bodies away from the water?"

The knowledge that these men had died horribly, with no trace of dignity or acknowledgement of their contributions to this world, caused Michael to feel a startling sensation of humility and respect. "Won't the tide wash them out to sea?"

Nevelle was walking more briskly now, a tinge of urgency adding weight to his words. "We can't stay here. If we don't hurry, these won't be the last victims we find tonight. This isn't the kind of behavior I've seen from this thing before. Something is different."

"Different how?" Michael raised an eyebrow and tried to ignore the gore all around him.

"I don't know, it just seems like he's..." Nevelle's voice trailed off for a moment. "Like he's trying to prove something."

The rumble of galloping horses could be heard coming from across the flat acre of rippling beach grass they'd just traversed.

"Get ready." Nevelle had one hand resting flatly on the pistol that hung from his belt.

An asymmetrical cascade of feral horses came barreling over the hill that partially blocked their sight of the plain beyond. They were mostly silhouettes in the moonlight, but the heavy panting that followed the shifting reverberation of their hooves left no doubt about what approached them.

Nevelle and Michael caught sight of the remainder of the hunting party. They had formed a mob, all drawn together by the frantic screams that punctuated this section of the island. Most of them ran with flashlights in hand, still a football-field's distance away, not slowing at the spectacle of the impending stampede.

The same roar they'd heard earlier that evening came rolling over the landscape like a monstrous call to order. The horses slid to a halt at the place where the vegetation gave way to the open beach. Then, from over the hill emerged the final horse of the herd. It was tough to tell what was happening at this distance, but an oblong, humanoid figure sat atop its back. The horse announced its presence with a strange whinny, an exclamation of obedience and anticipation.

"Holy hell," Nevelle whispered just as the remainder of the small throng of civil servants rounded the point. They ended their jog not far from where the Ranger stood.

It was immediately clear that the sasquatch had dispatched more of the volunteers and law enforcement personnel; Michael's best guess was that twelve–maybe thirteen–

people had survived. Now that they were closer, he could see that several were covered in blood, apparently not their own.

Bert Marshburn stood next to Clint. The pair turned to Nevelle and wordlessly acknowledged that yes, he had been right all along. Clint had been a fool not to heed the Ranger's warning.

"I know," was the only response Nevelle uttered.

Bert peered at the herd, which seemed inhumanly patient.

"Uh... is that..." His extended finger clearly singled out the strangely shaped horse that swayed at the apex of a grassy dune.

Nevelle nodded in disbelief. "Yeah. I think it is."

Michael then realized the absurdity of what they saw. The bigfoot was riding a horse and somehow commanded the herd that was fanned out before him.

The sasquatch raised an arm, its outline now distinct. The beast held an elongated object in its grip. An earth-shaking whoop momentarily caused the men to hold their breath.

What happened next could only be described as a beachfront bloodbath.

Chapter 10

A white horse trampled a young man as he fumbled with a handgun that should have been unholstered at least five seconds earlier. The sound of hoof keratin crushing the man's ribs somehow rose above the cacophony of gunshots that otherwise impeded Michael's ability to hear anything amid the garbled chaos.

The monster that led the charge clutched a thick section of mane, willing its steed forward with a "yawp!" that was caveman-like and guttural. Lowering his bone spear so that it was parallel to the ground, the monster assumed a joust stance. The creature was headed directly for Nevelle.

"Herman! Get the hell out of the way!" Clint ran as fast as he could, his age and weight limiting his progress. When the Deputy reached Nevelle, he shoved him to one side just as the Ranger had trained his gun on the beast.

An anguished cry rose from the battlefield, and Michael turned to see the Deputy being lifted from the sand and carried forward with the horse's momentum. The sasquatch pulled back on his mount, causing the horse to come about in a sharp half-circle.

Clint had been impaled in his chest, just above the left lung. He hollered and struggled against the weight of the weapon that held him, and, when the horse finally stopped, slid off and into the muddy expanse uncovered by the outgoing tide.

The bigfoot studied the Deputy for a moment. Clint winced and moaned, rolling across the wet ground, his right hand applying pressure to the wound. Though feeble, the attempt to stop the bleeding seemed–for the moment, at least–to be relatively successful. Just as the animal appeared poised to launch its spear directly at Clint's throat, a gunshot rang out. Nevelle had delivered a bullet to the creature's side, just under its raised arm. A howl of surprise followed, and the length of bone– now slick with blood–fell softly to the mud. The bigfoot spun around on the horse, one hand still clutching a tangle of hair, the other instinctively protecting the place it had been shot. Even in the muted light Michael could see the scarlet flowing down the beast's side.

When Nevelle locked eyes with his nemesis, the sasquatch dismounted and stood as straight as it could in the ebbing current.

"Get out of here." The Ranger turned to Michael. "This is going to be ugly."

Nevelle began walking forward at a steady clip, the shifting sand producing an uneven gait.

The bigfoot approached, its mass causing it to sink several inches with each step.

The ten or so remaining men on the beach surrounded the site of the showdown, the herd having mostly dispersed due to the gunfire and frantic shouting. Bert Marshburn and an older man with a thick, gray mustache approached the sasquatch. Michael thought the man with the mustache was the spitting image of Wilford Brimley.

Wilford leveled his shotgun and fired.

The buckshot caused a light spray of blood to plume into the night air from where it impacted the monster's chest. A low growl emanated from the beast. The sasquatch reached the man, picked him up by the throat, and squeezed. The high-pitched scream that followed quickly dissolved into a muddled squeal. From where they stood, the onlookers couldn't get off a clean shot. They nervously shifted in the sand, trying to achieve a better line of sight.

In the next instant, blood and matter ejected from Wilford's ears. Michael thought it looked like something he'd seen in an episode of Looney Tunes; a cartoon fire hydrant reaching maximum pressure and blowing its seals. The shock of the man's head exploding caused several of the men to stumble back.

The creature moved forward, still holding Wilford's lifeless body at arm's length as a shield. Bert ran toward the monster, yelling as loudly as he could, and swung a baseball bat he'd salvaged from the warzone in the direction of the creature's knees. The sasquatch snarled in pain when the Louisville Slugger made contact, stumbling but not dropping his victim. Instead, the bigfoot removed his other hand from the fresh bullet wound and placed it atop Bert's balding head. With a heavy effort, he issued a terrible caterwaul and pushed downward with all of his force. In a split-second, Bert became a revolting accordion; a sack of bones and organs that folded in upon itself. The collapsed, gelatinous remnants were driven two feet into the marshy terrain. The fiendish abomination continued its war march, his long-dead prey still hanging from the creature's closed fist and shifting with every footfall like a deformed dowsing rod.

Next came the white flag. Those who remained realized the futility of their efforts. One by one, they dropped their weapons: a rifle here, a crowbar there. The beach was littered with blood, bodies, and horses that had been wounded by panic fire. Like a flock of birds, those still lucky enough to be alive took flight in a reverse V formation. The survivors began their retreat as a slow jog that quickly evolved into a frantic sprint toward the landing where they prayed the ferry was waiting. It wasn't long before Nevelle, Michael, a gravely injured Clint, and a slightly hobbled sasquatch were all that remained.

"Get out of here, Mike." Nevelle forced a weak smile. "We've got this."

Michael didn't need to be told twice. Though he didn't want to abandon the man who had become a friend over the past twenty-four hours, he knew there was nothing more he could do. The desire for self-preservation took over, and, before his body could protest, Michael's brain was carrying him at full speed toward the waiting boat.

*   *   *

The Deputy rose to his feet, his blood-and-seawater-soaked shirt clinging to the place where the horse bone had punctured his chest and dislocated his shoulder. He did what he could to push the pain from his mind in order to concentrate on the task at hand.

Nevelle ejected the magazine from his handgun and examined it in the moonlight, confirming he had three rounds left. He slapped the clip in place, pulled back the slide, and watched as the monster pivoted between the two of them. Its eyes burned, and, for the first time in his handful of encounters with the beast, the Ranger could tell that it was in real, lasting pain.

"What's the play, Herman?" Clint stumbled and used one hand to push back the thin, wet hair at his forehead. "How many rounds you got?"

Nevelle gave him a nervous glance.

"Three." The Ranger widened his stance. "But we both know that won't do much."

"You gotta aim for the head."

It was a nice thought, but Nevelle suspected that the animal's skull was every bit as dense and well-proportioned as the rest of its physique.

"I'm not sure that's going to do anything, but I don't have any better suggestions."

The sasquatch locked its gaze on Clint and slowly began to take heavy steps toward the injured Deputy.

"When it grabs me, you shoot. You hear me? Get as close as you can and unload."

Nevelle's voice was tinged with sorrow. "Are you out of your mind? Run, man! RUN!"

Clint knew it was too late. The monster was hellbent on ending him, and there was nothing he could do to escape that fate. When the sasquatch reached the Deputy, it forced the man's arms apart. Huffman stood for a moment as a battered "T" in the rising surf, peering up at the face of this mythical thing that shouldn't be here.

"Come on, you son of a bitch!"

The bigfoot lifted him from the water, and, just when Clint could suddenly smell the putrid breath of the beast, he was unexpectedly dropped. The pain in his shoulder doubled with the impact, and the roiling waves made his attempts to get on his feet and stop himself from drowning a shockingly difficult challenge.

The Ranger had fired his first shot and hit the monster in the back of its wide head. The sasquatch stammered away from Clint, tripping over a sandbar and falling ass first into a tide pool.

The crack of another shot echoed across the beach.

Another direct hit, this time to the side of the beast's head.

The monster was clearly dazed, blood matting its hair and trailing down the unbelievably broad expanse of its shoulders.

The sasquatch placed both hands over its ears as if to squelch the pain that undoubtedly reverberated through its immense skull.

"Hit it again, Herman!" Clint had returned to the beach, absolutely worse for wear, barely able to stand. "AGAIN!"

Nevelle was closer to the animal now. At most, he was no more than ten feet from where the life seemed to be draining from the two bullet wounds in the creature's head and intermingling with the stagnant saltwater of the shallow pool it had collapsed into.

The Ranger carefully lined up his shot as he circled the beast, his feet crisscrossing methodically so as to maintain his balance. Nevelle wanted his final bullet to be delivered to the monster's forehead, and he was willing to get as close as he needed to.

Just as the Ranger squeezed the trigger, the monster lurched, quickly rising from the small pool.

A final shot rang out, and the animal immediately fell flat on its back. The heavy splat of its body cratered the moist sand and took the duo by surprise. Given the speed they'd observed that evening, they knew that once the bigfoot was in motion it would take a monumental effort and an exceptionally skilled marksman to land a fatal blow.

The Ranger cautiously approached the bigfoot. Its chest wasn't moving.

Upon closer inspection, he saw that blood flowed from its face. Then, in the waning glow from the moon, Nevelle saw what he'd done. The brute's left eye was gone. In its place was a black hole, dark blood spurting from it as a small geyser that steadily diminished.

"Holy shit, Herman. You killed it."

Clint moved closer.

"Damn it, Clint. Don't get near it. Quick—go find another gun. Check the beach. We need to be sure it's—"

The bigfoot was on its feet in a millisecond, and Clint was in its grasp. It had the man by a wrist, and he wriggled like a freshly caught chicken who knew it was about to be slaughtered.

"Christ! Clint!"

The animal picked up exactly where it had left off, gripping the Deputy's other arm at the wrist and returning him to the "T" pose Nevelle had seen just two minutes earlier.

"Run, Herman! Just get to the damn ferry!"

The Ranger dropped his gun and took off. He didn't look back when he heard the anguished cries of his friend and the awful tearing sound that overcame the ceaseless pulse of the Atlantic.

Chapter 11

The ferry had been late returning to the landing. In fact, the lines were just being cast off when Michael saw the shape of Nevelle become clear under the bulb of the lone telephone pole that jutted into the sky near the dock.

"Wait!" Michael hurried to the Captain, motioning toward the Ranger who coasted in on whatever fumes he had left in the tank.

When they pulled Nevelle aboard, exhaustion overcame him. He mumbled something about Clint; about shooting the monster. The other men who'd fled the beach crowded around Nevelle.

"It's still alive." The Ranger stated this as plainly as if he'd said, "water is wet."

"We're not done. This isn't over." Nevelle placed a hand on his head, squeezed his single eye shut, and broke into an uncontrollable sob. A hush fell over the ferry, and no one spoke again until the boat had cleared the waterway.

*   *   *

Thirty minutes later, they were idling alongside the port in Beaufort. Michael helped Nevelle to his feet.

The neon lights on the waterfront side of BOB's were a welcome sight, and Michael's phone began to ping with a flurry of notifications. Finally, he had acquired cell service and a stable signal. He glanced at his phone and saw that it was 5:08 AM.

With the aid of a lanky fisherman who helped secure the ferry when it arrived, Michael put Nevelle's right arm over his shoulder and walked the Ranger to a bench that sat flush with a painted brick wall facing the gravel lot.

When Michael got his companion seated and handed him a fresh bottle of water, he looked up to see Erica standing there, her arms folded, a palpable sadness causing her to seem small and worn beneath the flickering street lamp.

Michael slowly walked to her. When he saw Erica's face, he noted that her eyes were bloodshot. Dark crescents hung under both eyelids, and she only stared straight ahead.

"Erica." Michael didn't know what to say. "I..." he trailed off, issuing a quick glance toward Nevelle.

"You made the trip by yourself?"

Erica nodded and pulled a wadded Kleenex from her pocket. "Dad was going to come, but this just felt like something I needed to do by myself. I needed time to think." Her slender fingers placed two unruly locks of hair behind an ear. She silently nodded at the Ranger.

"Is he an officer? I was told I'd have to identify the remains." Her voice broke, and she used the tissue to dab at her eyes. A sudden anger overcame her and she jammed the Kleenex back into her pocket. "Just what the hell was he thinking, anyway!? Why was he obsessed with these little weekend adventures?"

"This wasn't his fault. He didn't do anything wrong." Michael stepped forward and hugged his friend. Frustration and the realization of what she still had to do caused her to step back in annoyance. "So, is that the guy I need to talk to?"

Nevelle was starting to come around. He stood, chugging the bottle of water, looking blankly at the gentle, oily ripples that collapsed against the pier under the soft lighting.

"No. He's a Park Ranger. He's the one who called you." A puzzled look fell over Erica's countenance. They listened to frantic voices crackle over a radio.

"HE'S HERE. OH MY GOD. HE'S–"

There was static followed by a sharp silence. At this point, several of the people who had been on the island and witnessed the evening's events had already made a beeline for their respective stations. There had been chatter about the FBI arriving at sunrise and returning to Shackleford, but no one seemed sure what, exactly, would happen next. The four officers who remained in the gravel lot appeared increasingly concerned by the sudden lack of radio communication.

Then an eerie stillness took over. For a moment, no one moved.

Erica pulled on Michael's arm. "What's going on here?"

Then, in the sporadic light produced by the bulb overhead, Michael caught a fleeting glimpse of the beast. It stood like a deranged swamp monster beneath the neon sign fastened to the corner of BOB's. It held a human head by the hair and stared, not much more than a shadow, its single eye the only thing visible in the predawn blackness.

*   *   *

When the bigfoot had finished removing the Deputy's arms from his torso, the creature held the man underwater with his giant right foot. He felt the human's body sinking into the muck, and eventually the man's legs went limp.

The creature's vision was clouded by a kaleidoscope of stars. His head pounded, and he was adjusting to sight with one eye. Though the irony of being partially blinded by his own cycloptic victim was not something the sasquatch was able to fully process, he was still stunned that, momentarily, he had been bested by these incredibly dull and inept beings.

Pain racked every inch of the beast's frame, and upon emerging from the surf, the monster dropped to one knee. He had to collect himself. This feeling of being overwhelmed was new. He was used to throttling his quarry with ease. Though there wasn't a definitive sense of looming death, the monster knew that no matter what, he had to push forward. Come sunrise, the humans would return in even greater numbers.

Breathing deeply, the creature righted himself and stood. The chill of an offshore breeze caused the wounds above and behind his ears to throb. His eye socket was a pulpy mess. The animal bent forward, scooped a handful of seawater from a nearby puddle, and splashed it on his partially mutilated face. The saltwater would help him heal, but it increased his pain tenfold. With an excruciating yelp, the bigfoot stumbled for a moment and then worked to regain his footing. Channeling his focus took every ounce of energy the animal had, but he knew this night wasn't over. He had set himself to a task, and he would see it through.

Now alone on the island, he ambled through the darkness toward the point. There, in the distance, his blurred night vision afforded him a view of the human settlement on the other side of the water. He swam the two and a half miles to reach this place once before, and he knew he could do it again. Still, there was no denying that he was badly injured. If he wasn't careful, he would drown in the rip current.

The sasquatch located an especially thick piece of driftwood. It was a knotted log about four feet in length, and he concluded it would serve his purpose well enough. His upper body ached continuously, and the baseball bat that had slammed into his knees hadn't done him any favors. All things considered, though, he felt as if his legs—machete wound and all—would hold up to the task of crossing the broad stretch of waterway.

Shackleford Banks Sasquatch

As he ventured into the breakers, the creature considered how he had arrived here. The malevolence of men, those small, ridiculous things that had, at one point, been a mere amusement. How they had persisted in trespassing on his land and driving him to the unknown reaches of the world. How he had narrowly avoided starvation and used his bottomless rage to continue onward.

When the sasquatch could no longer touch the silt beneath him with his feet, he leaned forward on the log. Now afloat, he churned his legs with everything he could muster. Soon he was gliding across the glassy inlet beyond the beach, his large, black marble of an eye laser-focused on the faraway lights of the small town he knew harbored the men that had tried to kill him.

*　　*　　*

Nevelle dropped the plastic water bottle onto the small rocks of the parking lot with a hollow thud.

"Run." He tried to say the word quietly, even though he knew the monster likely didn't understand its meaning.

Erica squinted, trying to discern what this hulking thing on the street corner was. When she saw the head it held more clearly, she brought a hand to her mouth and a barely audible squeak escaped her lips.

"Just back away. Keep backing up." Michael stood in front of Erica, slowly guiding her toward the open street where they would begin a mad dash toward somewhere more fortified.

The sasquatch kept its eye locked on Nevelle.

"He wants me. Seriously–go." Then, an idea. "Wait." Erica looked at the man as if he were insane.

"Get to the Seafarer Museum. I'll be there in ten minutes."

"Why?" Michael was confused and should have known better than to question the Ranger.

"Seriously? Just run. Get there as fast as you can."

Michael reached for Erica's hand, squeezed, and the pair bolted down the deserted, early morning street.

A tinge of orange had started to rise over the distant line of old brick buildings that made up downtown Beaufort.

"Yeah, I'm here you son of a bitch." The bigfoot stumbled for a moment, clutching at the corner siding of BOB's in an effort to steady itself.

Nevelle smiled. He knew that they had done some real damage to this thing and that it was taking everything the monster had to keep up the chase. Still, he'd seen what it was capable of far too often. He knew not to underestimate the bigfoot's will to butcher everything it encountered.

For the first time in his life, though, Herman Nevelle thought that he may actually be able to outrun the beast.

The sasquatch tossed the head it had removed from a hapless citizen onto the sidewalk. The Ranger observed that the flesh along the neck spiraled in a completely unnatural direction, as if the monster had turned his victim's cranium into a twist-off bottle cap.

Nevelle was feeling better now; he was no longer lightheaded and despondent, and the bottle of cold water had done him a world of good. Hurt or not, though, he knew there was no way he'd be able to take down this animal in a hand-to-hand fight. His pistol was out of ammo, and using his machete would result in a deep cut and the need for him to be dangerously close to this walking death machine.

He had a better idea.

Pursing his lips, he adjusted his backpack. After taking three quick breaths, Nevelle hurled himself into a full body sprint.

When he rounded the corner opposite BOB's, he dared not look over his shoulder. Any delay would likely cost him his life. The Ranger had to trust that the injuries he, Clint, and a bevy of other determined townspeople had dealt this thing was enough to give him the edge when it came to a flat-out footrace. His boots pounded the pavement, the echo of his soles ringing off nearby buildings. "Running shoes," he thought to himself when considering items to add to his pack. "I need some damn running shoes."

The Seafarer Museum was ahead and to the left. The entrance was well lit, and he could hear the blaring alarm system from fifty feet away. He saw that the glass of the front door had been shattered; Michael, he assumed, was already inside. Nevelle was glad his new friend hadn't hesitated in finding a way to enter the building as quickly as possible.

Nevelle ducked through the metal door frame and strode over the shards in the museum foyer.

"Mike!" The Ranger shout-whispered as he entered the building.

"How many times do I have to say it? It's Michael!" Erica and Michael shuffled over from behind an exhibit that featured a life-size Blackbeard.

The mannequin was full of detail, right down to the red ribbons tied in rows among its thick, black whiskers.

"Strip that thing down."

"What?" Michael looked at Nevelle like he was nuts.

"Trust me."

Erica was taking all of this in stride. The poor woman had just completed a cross-state, late night drive to identify the body of her dead husband, only to arrive at a scene of horror that featured a monster right out of a low-budget B movie. Michael couldn't help but admire how well she was processing everything.

Without an ounce of protest, Erica quickly removed the doublet, tricorn, and all other pirate garb adorning the mannequin. Michael had to wrestle with the wig and beard to pluck the things from the mannequin's head, but soon they were staring at a bald, completely-in-the-buff Edward Teach.

Nevelle returned from disabling the alarm and went to the gray breaker box.

"Time to kill the lights."

After throwing open the metal cover, he flipped a series of switches, and the place became completely and utterly dark. The sun was slowly creeping over the distant tree line in the windows, and Nevelle knew that the monster was close. He reached into his backpack and extracted what looked like a very cheap bigfoot costume.

"What the hell?" Nevelle handed the suit to Michael. "Did you buy this on Amazon?"

Nevelle smirked. "We don't have much time. Just put it on Blackbeard."

Erica helped squeeze the mannequin into the costume, and when they were finished, the duo couldn't help but chuckle at how stupid it looked.

"Okay, so, what the hell is actually going on here?" It was the first time Erica had spoken after seeing the creature, and Nevelle waved a dismissive hand.

"Listen, I am deeply sorry for your loss, but we have to focus. Set the mannequin in that corner."

The pair dragged the monstrosity into an especially dark place in the wings of the main atrium. Nevelle approached quickly, showing them a small vial.

"Bigfoot urine."

Michael furrowed his brow and snorted in disbelief.

Nevelle twisted off the small, black top and sprinkled the stuff on the decoy.

"Come on." He dragged the pair past a sloping wall. They were in another exhibit now; one that featured a small replica of a seventeenth century merchant ship. In a smaller, roped off area nearby were several cannons. The heavy guns were constructed of cast-iron and set on wooden blocks. Nevelle grunted as he unclasped one of the rope barriers and pivoted the armament toward the decoy.

"Here's something they don't tell you on the tour," he said in a low voice. "These things still work."

The Ranger jammed a waxy, exceptionally short section of what looked like rope into one end of the cannon. "Real pirates used a fuse called 'slow match.' This stuff is more...," he thought for a moment, "...modern. At this length, it'll burn to its end in about two seconds."

"Be right back." Nevelle trotted off briskly and vanished through a rear service door. He returned a few moments later with a lockbox. He turned the key and pulled back a square lid, revealing a black, granular substance and a piece of burlap.

"Gunpowder. Sometimes we give kids a little outdoor demonstration of how it works." Nevelle pointed to the cannon. "Help me tilt it back a bit." Michael placed both palms underneath the barrel and lifted the muzzle toward the rafters overhead. The Ranger poured in the powder and stuffed the wad of burlap in behind it. Then, using what looked like wool padding fastened to a stick, Nevelle jammed the contents in as far as they could go.

Nevelle fished a heavy cannonball out of the adjacent exhibit, and, eyeing its width, made sure it aligned with his weapon of choice. He dropped the ball in; Michael's arms were trembling with the weight of the cannon. The three of them held their breath as the ball rolled noisily toward the fuse. A soft clank echoed briefly in the wide, high-ceilinged room.

"Bullets can't kill it. Blades can't kill it. And I sure as hell can't get a license for an RPG." Nevelle laughed at the absurdity of the situation. "A cannon, though. That could do it. If a damn cannon can't kill it, then nothing short of a nuclear bomb is going to take this thing out."

A sudden quiet settled on the place, and Nevelle knew the time had come.

"I'm going out there." He was squatting and staring through the slowly dissolving darkness. "The scent will do the heavy lifting, but I need to make sure he goes for the bait." Nevelle pulled a small lighter from his backpack. "When he's two or three feet from the decoy, light the fuse. Don't hesitate. Just light it and cover your ears." Michael took the small Bic and tested it. A small spark followed by a wavering flame momentarily lit the exhibit.

With that, the Ranger shuffled off and found a shady spot near a large ship's wheel, about eight feet from the decoy.

If nothing else, Nevelle was right about the stench. Even from this distance Michael could smell the pungent stink that seemed to grow by the second. Erica held her nose and, for the moment at least, seemed to be locked into their goal. She watched the main door, and her knuckles were white as she held fast to the wooden rail in front of her.

For a minute, they heard nothing. Gulls signaled the sunrise in the distance, and the sounds of outbound fishing charters cut through the morning air.

Then the sasquatch arrived.

Chapter 12

Michael assumed the creature would enter through an unlocked window or backdoor in an attempt to catch them off guard. After all, stealth had been its calling card the world over for as long as the myth of this cryptid persisted.

Then he realized how dumb that was. This thing had abandoned subtlety earlier that same night, choosing to indiscriminately eviscerate throngs of people in full view of anyone who cared to watch. It was done being coy.

The monster had to duck as it moved through the rectangular door frame at the front of the building. In the twilight of dawn, it was a black mass that looked like a burly specter. It stepped on the broken glass, the pieces making soft cracking noises as it went. When the sasquatch was fully inside, it stopped and surveyed the scene.

Erica could hear it breathing. Its nose flared loudly, and the heat of its breath rose like a thin cloud of vapor. With a sudden jerk of its head, it looked toward the decoy.

A sense of disbelief and confusion appeared to move the thing forward. Its hands were open, flat at its sides, and the behemoth seemed cautious. Even so, the scent was doing its work; the bigfoot couldn't resist the smell of its species. It drew near and soon became a looming target. Both Erica and Michael could see that the brute was limping as it walked. The sasquatch was coated in blood and tangles of seaweed were caught in its fur.

As quietly as he could, Michael, his hands suddenly perspiring, raised the lighter toward the crude fuse Nevelle had fashioned at the stock of the cannon.

Erica's hand slipped on the rail, and a brief screech splintered the silence. The sasquatch whipped its head around. Michael's heart sank, and he gripped his friend's arm.

Just as the monster turned toward the pair, Nevelle arose from behind the giant, eight-spoked wheel.

"So, you're the reigning hide and seek champion of the world, eh?"

The creature jerked in surprise, its attention now fixed on the Ranger. Nevelle moved toward the decoy. The monster's breathing intensified, and it suddenly accelerated its place, arms extended, ready to dismantle the human who had so persistently tried to end its existence.

Erica pinched Michael, and he realized the animal, with its massive stride, had suddenly entered the kill zone. For a moment, Michael thought of Tom, his lifelong friend, and how much he would have enjoyed all the maritime antiquities this place had to offer.

Nevelle grinned and spat out a one-liner he'd been holding on to for a long, long time.

"Peek-a-boo, motherfucker."

With a flick of the lighter, the cannon fuse fizzled, sparked briefly, and released an ear-splitting boom.

*   *   *

Upon entering this structure, the bigfoot was unsure of how to process its surroundings. The pain had grown more intense since the earlier events of the evening, and the wounds that circled its head and legs had evolved into stupendous points of anguish. When he tried to summon his usual speed to ensnare the fleeing human, his body simply said, "No."

He would do this slowly, then, and with resolve, as he had done so many other things.

Then there was his destroyed eye. His night vision was sharp, but the blur of agony he contended with made it difficult to focus. The cryptid knew that at least one human was here–the human he had been seeking.

Despite his ailments, the animal's nose still picked up on scents from miles away. When the unmistakable odor of his family unit made it to him, the swell of emotion he felt almost knocked him over. He hadn't encountered this since they'd been split apart in the forest all those years ago, and he didn't imagine he'd ever find them again.

Then he saw it: an outline to match the smell. He observed the ruffled hair and elongated face; the motionless stare that his kind were required to perfect in order to dissolve among the trees. He approached cautiously, juggling both hope and disbelief. He raised a single bloody hand, this unprecedented reunion something he could have never predicted.

Then a sound of disorder; bleating and sloppy. A man. One of those creatures that afflicted his daily reality. The unchecked anger that he'd felt for so long returned with an otherworldly force.

From near his kin, a new revelation: the human he'd been determined to end, finally and definitively, before the next sunrise. The creature stared at him, one single-eyed being confronting another. The monster knew he had to choke the life out of his man. He sensed an ambush, but the bigfoot wouldn't be deterred. The pain he worked to keep at bay and the smell of his long-absent clan collided in his brain and caused confusion.

But the human was right there. He could make one last push to close the gap.

When the sasquatch finally cordoned off the pain and found the strength for his final effort, he was surprised at the thunderous sound that seemed to arise from nowhere and everywhere.

Chapter 13

When the early eighteenth-century cannonball tore through the sasquatch, the aftermath wasn't immediately visible because of the heavy smoke that lingered in the room. Michael's ears were ringing, and he was doubled over in a coughing fit. Erica stared in disbelief, clumsily trying to stand after the recoil from the cannon broke the rail at her side and tossed her to the floor.

When Michael found his breath, he made his way into the atrium and saw that Nevelle was stunned but alive. The Ranger was a blood-spattered mess; chunks of flesh and hair clung to him, and his lone eye was blinking rapidly to try and dispel any debris. Michael then saw that the cannonball had blasted a jagged hole in the side of the museum. Daylight streamed in, and cars had stopped in the middle of the street. Onlookers slowly approached the smoking hole to get a better view of what had just erupted from one of downtown Beaufort's most recognizable attractions.

When they'd gathered themselves and Erica joined the men in the large room, the trio saw the result of their work. The sasquatch had been ripped in half by the ancient munition; literally split in two at the waist. Nevelle picked up a nearby stool, sat it upright, and lowered himself onto the seat.

"Can y'all hear me?" The Ranger stuck a pinky in one ear and seemed to bite his tongue. "Jesus, that was way louder than I expected. I think I used too much powder."

"Did we just kill Bigfoot?" Erica asked the obvious question, her hands on her hips as she craned for a view of the creature's face.

"As a matter of fact, I think we did. A bigfoot, anyway." Nevelle exhaled loudly and placed both hands on his knees.

Michael began scratching his head as he realized the futility of trying to make sense of the sheer lunacy he'd encountered over the past twenty-four hours.

"So, what now?"

Nevelle thought for a moment and stood. He extended a hand to Michael, who took it and shook slowly.

"There are more of them. That sasquatch piss I used–" Nevelle pulled the empty vial from this pocket. "I collected this in the Uwharrie; found it in one of two nests." He held the small tube between his index finger and thumb. "The SBI dismissed it as having come from a bear, but you saw how that thing reacted to the smell. And now we have proof."

They turned to the partially charred corpse that lay in two great heaps on the tile of the museum floor.

"This is going to change the world."

Chapter 14

Erica spread Tom's ashes near a waterfall along the Virginia Creeper Trail that October. Her husband had loved his annual bike excursions to the area, and she knew this was where he'd want to spend eternity. There was a serenity and calm that Michael observed as young people on bikes raced by thirty feet away, their wheels whirring in the cold fall air. Leaves the color of fire trailed them in great plumes as they went.

"This was a good choice," Michael told Erica as she delicately emptied the container. The rush of water created a hovering mist above the pool at the base of the falls. Their own bikes were propped against two twisting oaks just off the paved pathway. They had about two more hours of biking before they made it back to their rental car and began the winding afternoon drive to North Carolina.

When the pair returned to their bikes, Michael couldn't help peering over his shoulder. He knew something was out there, watching. Perhaps it didn't yet have a reason to hate humanity. "This place," he thought, "It's isolated enough."

But Michael knew things wouldn't always be that way. Eventually, a collision would happen. One of these eager bicyclists would stumble upon a primeval entity, and a trajectory of terror would descend up an otherwise sleepy corner of Virginia.

Since they'd uncovered the existence of a mythical beast that had been long considered an elaborate hoax, primatologists and anthropologists issued warnings about what it all meant. Clashing ecosystems. Territorial disputes. Grisly encounters that might have no end.

For now, though, Michael found a strange solace in the knowledge that things were in balance. The scales were even, and maybe this prehistoric species would maintain its distance. "Maybe they're going extinct," he mused. "After all, the Shackleford Bigfoot is the only indisputable proof that these things are real. There haven't been any others."

In his gut, though, Michael knew this was only the beginning. After eons of silence, something had been awakened.

A time of doubt had evolved into an era of belief.